DRAW-IT-YOURSELF ADVENTURES

SPY MISSION

ANDREW JUDGE & CHRIS JUDGE

Little, Brown and Company
New York Boston

PSSST!

You!

Yes, **YOU**, the kid reading this book.

I have a **SECRET MISSION FOR YOU!**

But first find something to **DRAW** with and then I'll explain.

 Check here when you have a pencil.

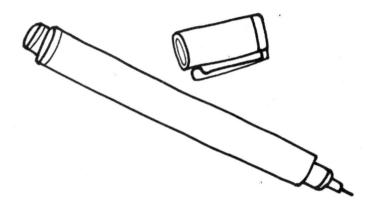

So what else does it do?

It shoots poison darts.

It's a secret radio.

Actually, it just draws lines.

Let's test your pencil.

Do a quick drawing of a **MUFFIN** here:

Great work.

You had better get used to drawing because
this book is filled with

HALF-DRAWN ADVENTURE!
and
INCOMPLETE ACTION!

So what's this book about?

Good question. It's about **SPIES**.

And Doodles.

Doodles are half-started, but not fully finished, drawings.

In this story you will also have to **FOLD** pages and even **RIP OUT** pages.

Let's try that out now.

FOLD THE
PAGE HERE.

Now turn to page 137.

Finally, this book is about a **TOP SECRET** mission.

Do you think you can keep a secret?

 YES   Great. Now turn the page and let's start!

 NO   Oh dear. Turn to page 134.

CHAPTER ONE
MISSION!

If you were on a plane and needed to get off quickly, would you do this?

YES, obviously, if you were **ETHAN DOODLE**, super spy!

Welcome to the world of Ethan Doodle.

No **THRILL** is too thrilling!

No **DANGER** is too dangerous!

No **PARACHUTE** is...bad.

"**AAAAAARGH!** I forgot to pack one!" says Ethan.

This is going to be a very short book unless you can help him out. You had better draw a parachute to save him or he will need to change his name to Ethan Doodle, Super Splat!

Phew! Okay, so where were we?

Oh, yes: Ethan. Falling.

This is a very exciting start, isn't it? I bet you are wondering **WHAT** is going on.

Well, I can tell you this: See that train at the bottom of the page? Ethan needs to get on board it as quickly as possible before it goes into the tunnel on the opposite page.

Ethan lands on the roof of the train and sees that it is about to go into the tunnel. If he doesn't do something quickly he's going to be splattered like a bug on a windshield.

Ethan runs along the roof and then **LEAPS** off. He grabs on to the side and swings through an **OPEN** window.

Oops! I forgot to mention you need to **DRAW** an open window for him to swing through. Quick!

Ethan gets on board the train. He needs to get to the other end of it as quickly as possible. It's an **EMERGENCY**! He runs through the train car. He leaps over a big suitcase in the aisle.

He crawls along the luggage rack to avoid a crying baby.

DRAW UNDRAWN JOHN HERE!

He crawls under a seat because, well, it's more exciting than just running down the aisle.

He stops to get a cup of juice from the snack cart. A cup of juice? What are you doing, Ethan? This is no time for juice. It's an **EMERGENCY**!

Ethan finally reaches the **BATHROOM** at the other end of the train.

Yes, it's **THAT** kind of emergency.

But it looks like the bathroom is occupied. Oh no, this is a disaster! Unless...

Quick! Change the sign to **UNOCCUPIED** while no one is looking.

Nice job! Emergency averted! You saved the day!

"Phew," says Ethan. "That was close. Another ten seconds and I would have ▬▬▬ my ▬▬▬▬."

Yes, well, thank you very much for that information, Ethan. I'm sure we all needed to know that. Thank goodness this is a book about **SPIES** because that will hopefully be **BLACKED OUT** before it is printed.

Right there

Ethan looks around the bathroom. "Um, there's no toilet paper..."

Just when you thought this book could not get any more exciting.

CHAPTER TWO
MUFFINS!

Let's get on with the story.

The train is heading toward Doodletown, and it's not long before fields and hills give way to buildings and bridges. The train approaches the station and pulls up alongside the platform. But look! The track isn't fixed yet!

Quick! Finish drawing the tracks!

DOODLETOWN

DRAW MORE TRACKS!

Ethan gets off the train and heads for the exit. He has a busy day of action-packed spy stuff ahead of him.

"Okay," says Ethan. "Shopping first, then coffee."
See what I mean? Action-packed.

Ethan has a lot of things to do today. But most important is a visit to his favorite shop:

SELF-DESTRUCTOR
BAG

I ♥ SPYING
T-SHIRTS

THROWING HAT
(HANDLE WITH CARE)

X-RAY BINOCULARS

COFFEE MACHINE
(JUST MAKES COFFEE)

You need wall-climbing gloves?
No problem, you can get them here.
Disguises?
X-ray glasses?
Tiny cameras?
This shop has everything.

WALL-CLIMBING
GLOVES

Ethan is here to pick up essential supplies.

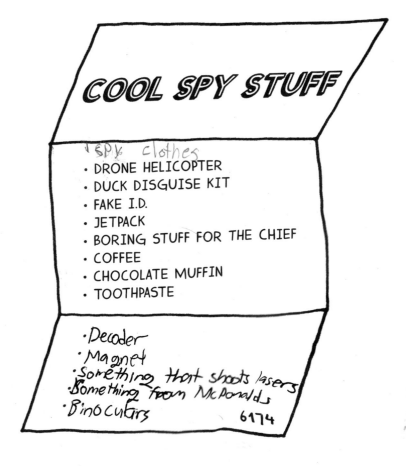

COOL SPY STUFF

spy clothes

- DRONE HELICOPTER
- DUCK DISGUISE KIT
- FAKE I.D.
- JETPACK
- BORING STUFF FOR THE CHIEF
- COFFEE
- CHOCOLATE MUFFIN
- TOOTHPASTE

- Decoder
- Magnet
- Something that shoots lasers
- Something from McDonalds
- Binoculars   6174

Maybe you can think of some more **COOL STUFF** to add to the list. What else would a spy need?

Ethan opens the door and enters. The shop is filled with awesome gear. There are twelve different types of **BINOCULARS** hanging from the ceiling. There is a cabinet filled with **FALSE MUSTACHES** and shelves piled high with **DART PENS**, **JETPACKS**, and **NINJA** supplies.

At the back of the shop, Ethan is met by the owner and his mysterious assistant.

DRAW SOME STUFF ON THE SHELVES.

"Good morning, Mr. Sonley," *says* Ethan.

"I'm not Mr. Sonley," says the *person* on the left. "I'm his wife. That's Mr. Sonley." She *points* to the person on the right.

"Shh, dear!" says the person on the right. "Don't tell everyone."

Mr. Sonley takes off his clever mask.

"Nice disguise, Mr. Sonley," says Ethan. "I would hardly have recognized you."

Mr. Sonley nods. "Thank you, Ethan. I impress myself sometimes. How can I help you today?"

"My usual supplies." Ethan hands him the list. "Anything new to show me?"

Mr. Sonley gives him a smile. "Indeed. Follow me. I have something **EXCELLENT** to show you."

He invites Ethan into the back of the shop through the secret door that is **SO** secret it's **NOT EVEN THERE**.

Some time later...

Ha! I bet you were expecting me to tell you what the excellent thing is? **NO CHANCE!** You'll just have to wait.

"I can't wait to try out the excellent thing Mr. Sonley gave me," says Ethan, teasing you even more.

And so, on with the...

AWESOME, ACTION-PACKED ADVENTURE!

But first, a coffee.

Ethan makes his way to McGuffin's Muffins, the home of the best muffins in the world. After Spies 'R' Us, this is Ethan's second-favorite place to visit because they make a blueberry chocolate chip banana muffin, which is **DELICIOUS!**

What's your favorite muffin? Draw it and color it in.

That ?? Maffin

When Ethan's muffin arrives, he decides to **SHARE IT** with the world. You can't have one and not **TELL EVERYONE**, after all!

Ethan takes a photo of the muffin and uploads it to Spyrock, his favorite espionage network. Soon he has over one million "likes" and he hasn't even touched his coffee yet.

Ethan is sitting there reading all the hilarious comments from his friends about his muffin when suddenly the kitchen door at the back of the coffee shop **BURSTS** open!

KER-RASH! Tables and chairs and cups and saucers and plates go flying as Mr. Dozen, the baker, comes charging out of the kitchen waving his arms!

"It's **GONE**!" he screams. "My muffin recipe is gone!"

DRAW MORE STAINS.

It's a **DISASTER**!
The apron, I mean.

MAYHEM! Everybody in the coffee shop panics. McGuffin's Muffins with no muffins? It's unthinkable.

A grown man starts crying. An old lady falls off her chair. A baby starts to wail. Two teenagers start texting each other. The waitress quits her job.

31

CHAPTER THREE

SPIES!

The McGuffin muffin recipe has been stolen! Who could have committed this **AWFUL** crime?

Ethan **LEAPS** into action!

He **STARES** at his phone intently for a couple of minutes.

This is very **EXCITING**, isn't it?

He does some more staring and scrolling. He taps something and then uses two fingers to zoom in.

He turns his phone sideways and then up the right way again. Thrilling stuff, eh?

Actually, he **IS** doing something very smart and useful. He is going through the photos on his phone to see if there are any **HINTS**. Maybe he took a picture of the person who stole the recipe?

If you think it was this guy, then turn to page 34.

Maybe it was this lady? Turn to page 44.

Or was it this man? Turn to page 58.

Ethan runs outside. He is searching for the Man with the Newspaper—but there is no sign of him. He must have slipped away during the chaos in the coffee shop. He can't have gone far, though. Can **YOU** spot him?

Ethan pulls out his phone again and opens the Trackr app. He uploads the photo of the Man with the Newspaper and presses FIND. A few seconds pass and then the Man's location pops up on the screen.

Draw a line to show Ethan the way to go.

Ethan races along the street. The Man with the Newspaper went this way. He can't be far.

Sure enough, Ethan soon spots him. He's getting rid of his newspaper.

This guy is smart, thinks Ethan. He's disguised himself as a Man **WITHOUT** the Newspaper.

Ethan takes the newspaper from the trash can. He pokes two holes in the page and pretends to read it as he keeps following the Man without the Newspaper.

NEWS

POKE TWO EYEHOLES IN THE PAGE WITH YOUR PENCIL.

SPACESHIP
SKIMS SCHOOL

NEAR-MISS MYSTERY

SPORTS

DOODLETOWN DRAWS WITH CRAYONS

DOODLETOWN UNITED 1
CRAYON CITY 1

The Man's phone rings and he answers it. Ethan gets closer so that he can hear what is being said.

"Yes," the Man is saying, "I've got it." He nods as he listens. "No problem. I will be there shortly. I think he will be very happy."

The Man finishes the call and continues down the street.

Very suspicious, thinks Ethan as he continues to follow him.

The Man makes his way across town.

Look where he is going! It's...

Ethan watches as the Man without the Newspaper
passes through the gates and into the factory.
Ethan needs to follow him.

"**STOP!**" A big security guard blocks Ethan's way.
"No admittance without authorization," says the guard.

Ethan thinks quickly. "No problem," he says. "I
have it right here." He needs to bluff his way into the
factory. Luckily he is a spy and has some fake I.D.
cards.

Which **TITLE** should he use?

☐ Cake Inspector

☑ Muffin Grandmaster

☐ Mr. Flakey's Cousin

40

"Thank you, Mr. Katz," says the security guard, looking at the fake I.D. "Is Mr. Flakey expecting you?"

Ethan shakes his head. "No. It's a surprise visit."

"Ah, I see," says the security guard, tapping the side of his nose. "The big secret. Don't worry, I won't let him know you've arrived."

Very mysterious!

Inside, Ethan explores the gigantic cake factory. He passes huge silos filled with flour, under pipes full of milk and chocolate. He passes a giant mountain of sugar and a warehouse full of eggs. He spots the Man without the Newspaper slipping through a door into a side building.

Ethan follows him. He finds himself in a brightly lit stairwell. He can hear the Man climbing the stairs above him. He follows him quietly upward to...

...the office of Mr. Flakey **HIMSELF**!

That must be it! The Man without the Newspaper is a **SPY**! Mr. Flakey has asked him to steal the **BEST MUFFIN RECIPE EVER**!

Ethan pulls his camera out of his bag and takes a photo for evidence.

"Excuse me, Mr. Katz?"

Ethan isn't paying attention and doesn't hear the security guard come up behind him. He jumps with fright.

"You left your I.D. card behind," says the security guard.

"Who's there?" says a voice from inside the office.

"It's me, Mr. Flakey. Frank the security guard."

Mr. Flakey steps out of the office to see Frank and Ethan. "Hello, Frank," he says. He looks at Ethan. "Who's this?"

"**SURPRISE!**" says Frank. "It's Mr. Katz!"

Mr. Flakey stares at Ethan. Mr. Flakey stares at Ethan's camera. "Frank," says Mr. Flakey, "you are the **WORST** security guard **EVER**. I told you not to let people sneak around my factory with a camera." He turns to Ethan. "I'm not sure what you are doing, Mr. Katz, but I don't like it."

"Do you expect me to talk?" asks Ethan.

"No, Mr. Katz," says Mr. Flakey with an **EVIL** laugh. "I expect you to **LEAVE QUIETLY.**"

"And, Frank," says Mr. Flakey sternly. "No complimentary Flakey Cakes for him on the way out, okay?"

Now turn to page 70.

While everyone else screams and panics, Ethan watches as the Mysterious Lady in the Polka-Dot Blouse quietly stands up and walks out of the coffee shop. He grabs his bag and heads out the door behind her. She is standing on the curb, waving down a taxi.

The taxi pulls up, the Mysterious Lady gets in, and it speeds off. Ethan hurries to the next taxi and jumps in.

He yells at the driver. "Quick! Follow that cab!"

"Hooray!" says the driver. "I've been waiting fifteen years for someone to say that."

The taxi driver races to keep up. They head along Doodletown's main street and take a sharp right.

They zoom through Chinatown past Ethan's favorite restaurant, the Wok & Roll Café.
Dim sum!

They zoom past Doodletown Library, which reminds Ethan he has some late books to give back.

Ethan spots a shortcut.
"Go down that alley to catch them," he says to the driver.

He's right! Draw a line to show the driver the way down the alley.
Don't bump the walls!

Ethan's taxi emerges from the alley on to the street. There is the other taxi just in front of them. Good shortcut!

The traffic is heavier here. Both cars slow down to a crawl and eventually come to a stop. A heavy traffic jam fills the middle of the page, with a variety of cars, trucks, and buses.

Ethan's taxi is just behind the Mysterious Lady's.

Ethan watches as the Mysterious Lady's taxi pulls up to the curb and she steps out. She sets off down the sidewalk.

"Let me out here, thanks," says Ethan. "How much is the fare?"

The driver pulls over to the curb and points to the meter. "That will be ten doodlers, mate."

Ethan checks his wallet for cash. It's **EMPTY**! He spent all his money on spy gear and muffins.

Ahem. We shouldn't really do this, but do you think you could **DRAW** some money for Ethan?

That's pretty impressive!

The driver takes the money and holds it up to the light.

Seems legit!

"Keep the change," says Ethan as he hops out of the cab.

Ethan runs to catch up with the Mysterious Lady. She walks down the street until she reaches a rack of rental bikes. She swipes her card and pulls one out.

She mounts up and cycles away.

Ethan runs over to get a bike.

Ethan jumps on to a bike and sets off, following the Mysterious Lady on the Bicycle through the park.

This is the life! Mystery! Thrills! Fresh air!

These free rental bikes are great, he thinks. But they are a bit boring.

He's right. The bike is not very **SPY-TASTIC**.

Maybe you could improve it a bit?

DRAW HELICOPTER WINGS.

DRAW A LASER.

ADD A ROCKET BOOSTER.

ADD MUDGUARDS WITH MISSILES.

Great work, the bike looks **AWESOME** now.

Not very subtle, but **AWESOME** nonetheless.

Ethan races after the Mysterious Lady and finally catches up with her just as she arrives at her destination.

This explains a lot! It's a bakery called...

And she's Kate of Kate's Baked Cupcakes! Try saying that quickly.

Ethan watches as Kate returns the bike to a rental-bikes stand and goes into her cupcake shop. Maybe she stole the famous McGuffin muffin recipe for her own bakery?

We've **GOT** to find out!

Ethan spots an alley beside the cupcake shop and sneaks down it to see if there is a back door.

He finds one but it is securely locked.

He looks for an open window but they are all tightly closed.

He looks for a way onto the roof, but there is no drainpipe to climb.

He sits down beneath the big kitchen extractor fan, which drones away noisily. There must be some way to get a look inside, he thinks.

Ahem! **DRONES** away noisily…

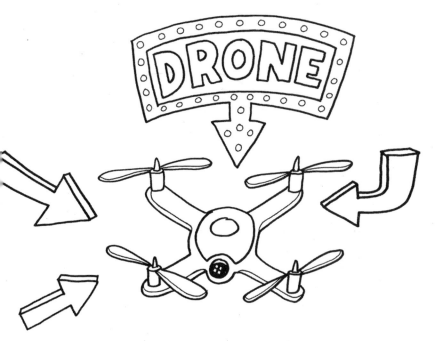

"Of course," Ethan says aloud. "My micro-drone!"

Ethan takes his micro-drone from his backpack.

(No, this isn't the excellent thing Mr. Sonley gave him earlier. That comes later!)

He sets the drone on the ground. Using the remote control, he starts it up. The rotors spin faster and faster and the drone lifts off the ground. Ethan pilots it toward the extractor fan outlet. The fan inside is spinning quickly, but if he can fly the drone **JUST RIGHT** he can get inside.

Once past the fan, Ethan has to fly the drone carefully through the maze of ductwork to the kitchen. Draw the route for him, making sure the drone doesn't touch the sides of the pipes.

Good flying! The drone reaches a grill in the kitchen wall and hovers there quietly. He watches the scene on the remote-control screen. He can see Kate preparing to bake. She has bowls and flour and eggs and sugar and mixers on the kitchen counter. It looks like she is getting ready to make **MUFFINS**.

But whose recipe is she using?

Ethan sees someone else enter the kitchen. Kate says something to him, but Ethan cannot hear it. He realizes that the volume knob on the drone is turned off.

Set the volume to 11 so that Ethan can hear what is being said.

"...should definitely win the baking contest," Kate is saying.

Her colleague leans against the counter. "But the competition is really tough this year."

"I've got a secret weapon this time," says Kate. "I've got a **NEW** recipe."

I need to record this and take some photos as evidence, thinks Ethan. He tries to press RECORD, take some **PHOTOS**, and fly the **DRONE** all at the same time.

Try it yourself. It's not so easy, is it?

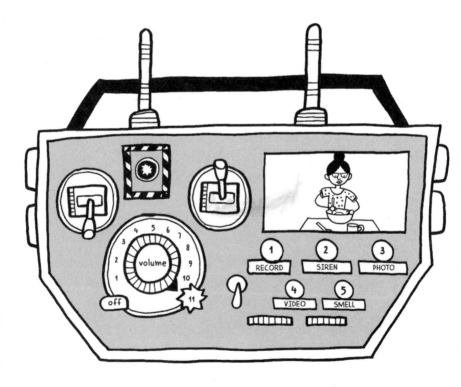

As Ethan tries to do everything at the same time the drone wobbles and bumps into the wall. It goes out of control and bounces around the duct.

KER-RANG! SP-TANG! PI-CHING!

Kate looks up at the duct in surprise. "What the...?" she gasps.

Ethan's cover is compromised! Disengage!

In a panic he presses the SELF-DESTRUCT button.

That was a bit drastic, Ethan. You've wrecked the place!

Ethan runs from the scene, leaving a very confused Kate behind.

Blowing up a bakery was not on Ethan's list of **THINGS TO DO TODAY**.

Still, a good spy needs to be adaptable, I suppose.

Now turn to page 70.

While everyone runs around in a panic, Ethan watches as the Old Man leaves the coffee shop. Ethan decides to follow him and see where he goes.

But first he needs to put on a disguise so that he will not be too obvious.

Select a disguise for Ethan and draw it on him.

Outside, the Old Man walks slowly down the street. As Ethan follows him, the man pulls a piece of crumpled paper from his pocket, unfolds it, and starts to read.

Ethan needs to see what it says.

Go to page 135 to get some binoculars.

Did you get the binoculars? Have a look at page 143 to see what the paper says.

Ethan follows the Old Man to the supermarket.

Inside they make their way to the **BAKING AISLE. OMG!** The Old Man suddenly turns to Ethan. Ethan immediately pretends to be very interested in raisins.

"Excuse me," says the Old Man. "Can you read my list? I left my glasses at home."

Ethan takes the paper and reads the list aloud. "Do you want me to help you with these?" he asks.

"That would be very kind of you," says the Old Man.

Help him by drawing the missing ingredients.

This is Ethan's chance to find out more!

"Are you doing some baking?" he asks, trying to sound casual.

The Old Man nods. "Yes. It's an old family recipe that I've been using for years."

Ethan looks at him suspiciously. "Then what do you need an ingredients list for?"

The Old Man gets flustered. "It's...well...I must be going now. Thank you." The Old Man turns and hurries away but leaves his shopping basket behind.

"Wait," Ethan calls after him. "You forgot your ingredients."

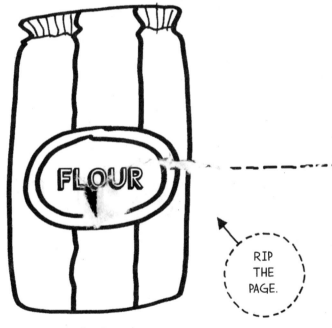

FLOUR

RIP
THE
PAGE.

Quick! Rip a small hole in the bag!

The Old Man turns, takes the basket from Ethan, muttering, "Thank you," and hurries away.

Ethan follows him to the checkout. The Old Man uses the express lane while Ethan gets stuck behind a lady buying thirty cans of cat food and paying for it in coupons.

When he eventually gets outside the Old Man is **GONE**!

Luckily you made a hole in the bag. There is a trail of flour to follow!

The trail of flour leads to a big house. I mean a **REALLY** big house. A **REALLY** big house with a high wall around it and an overgrown garden filled with trees.

Ethan follows the trail through the gates and up to the front door, which is locked.

But Ethan is a spy and spies always have a **MASTER KEY** with them. A master key opens **ANY** lock.

Can you draw a master key for Ethan?

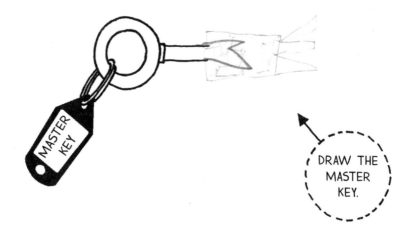

DRAW THE
MASTER
KEY.

Ethan lets himself quietly into the house. He sneaks
down the hallway. On the wall he sees a large
painting.

Ethan suddenly realizes who the Old Man is.

"Of course!" he says aloud. "It's Lord Byron de Doodle."

The de Doodle family is, of course, one of the oldest families in Doodletown, and Lord Byron is the last surviving member.

Once he was a dashing figure in Doodletown, who attended garden parties and danced with the ladies. He was famous for his racing ducks, who won the Doodle Duck Derby every year.

Then one day Crackers, his favorite duck, was **SQUISHED** by a steamroller just after winning the famous Duck of York Cup Race. Lord Byron was so heartbroken that he locked himself away in his home and was never seen again.

Until now, that is.

Ethan hears a noise at the back of the house. It sounds like it's coming from the **KITCHEN**.

Draw a line to show Ethan the way to the kitchen.

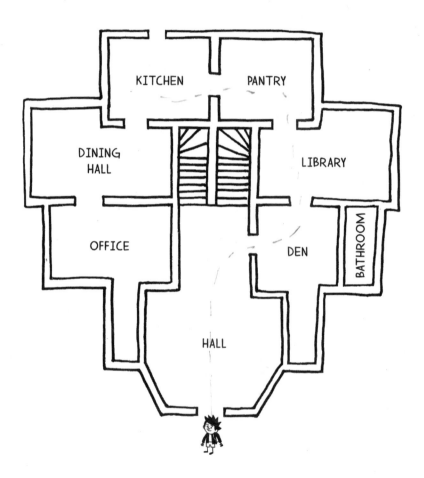

Ethan moves through the rooms and peeps around a door.

The kitchen is a big, old room with a large stove on the opposite wall. There is a wooden table in the center. Lots of bowls are laid on the table and wooden spoons are hanging from the ceiling.

Lord Byron stands at the table wearing an apron and mixing a bowl of ingredients.

Ethan watches as he pours the contents of the bowl into a large baking tray and places it in the oven.

After Lord Byron leaves the room by the back door, Ethan sneaks into the kitchen and takes a look at what Lord Byron is baking.

I knew it! Muffins!

Ethan hears the back door opening and jumps into the pantry to hide. He watches through a crack in the door as Lord Byron takes the muffins out of the oven and places them on a cooling rack, then carries it outside.

Ethan slips out behind Lord Byron and follows him through the garden until they reach the **DUCK POND**. Lord Byron starts breaking off bits of muffin and throwing them into the pond. The ducks begin to feed.

"Do you like them, my lovelies?" says Lord Byron to the ducks. "These are the ones I'm entering in the **BAKING CONTEST**."

Time to get a sample, thinks Ethan.

He pulls his wetsuit and snorkel from his backpack and puts them on. Thank goodness he picked up that duck disguise in the Spies 'R' Us!

He slips into the water and swims among the ducks. Lord Byron throws more muffins.

"**QUACK! QUACK! QUACK!**" shouts Ethan. The other ducks scatter in fright. Lord Byron squints and then shrugs his shoulders. He still hasn't found his glasses.

Ethan grabs a piece of soggy muffin in his mouth. It's disgusting. "Urgh!" He swims back to the shore, climbs out, and carefully slips the piece of muffin into a plastic bag.

DRAW A DUCK ON ETHAN'S HEAD.

CHAPTER FOUR
TROUBLE!

When Ethan returns to the scene of the crime with his evidence, he finds McGuffin's Muffins surrounded by police cars. A police helicopter circles overhead. The police in Doodletown treat a Felony #263 (Baked Goods Crime) **VERY SERIOUSLY**.

Ethan sees Mr. Dozen, the baker, talking to Police Detective Spiral. "I know who did it!" he says as he approaches them.

Mr. Dozen and Detective Spiral turn to Ethan.

"So do we," says Detective Spiral. "You are under arrest, Ethan Doodle!"

Two policemen grab Ethan by the arms.

Detective Spiral holds up a picture. "Is this your drawing?"

Turn to page 7 to see the drawing.

71

"Yes, that's mine," says Ethan, "but it's not what you think."

Detective Spiral glares at him. "You can explain that to the **JUDGE**. Take him away."

The two policemen march Ethan out of the coffee shop and into the backseat of a police car.

At the police station, Detective Spiral questions Ethan:

"Why did you do this drawing?"

"Why did you leave McGuffin's Muffins in a hurry?"

"Why do you have a backpack full of disguises?"

The questions go on for **AGES**, like when your parents ask you about school after you get home.

"I didn't steal the recipe, but I know who did," says Ethan. "I can draw them for you."

Detective Spiral reluctantly agrees to let Ethan use the identikit. "Okay," he says, "show me who **DID** steal it and we'll see."

Draw the suspect on the next page.

IDENTIKIT

Detective Spiral is intrigued by the picture. "I will look into this," he says. "But you are not off the hook yet, Ethan." He turns to the other policeman. "Lock him in a cell until we get to the bottom of this."

Ethan starts marking off his time in prison on the cell wall.

One minute. Two minutes. Three minutes. Four minutes.

After twenty-four minutes he has had enough.

He looks around the cell for a way out. But the door
is tightly locked and the window has thick bars on it.

But luckily, this book is made out of paper!

You can help Ethan escape by ripping the page just
there!

Ethan climbs through the rip in the page and...

...out into the police station parking lot. There are thirty police cars. One of the police officers sees him escaping and blows his whistle.

PHWEEEEEEEEEEEEEEEE!

Ethan drops down from the rip in the wall and quickly pulls his skateboard from his backpack.

He pushes off and skates out on to the street. Twenty-nine police cars immediately start chasing him.

The other one has a flat tire.

Ethan races down the street. One of the police cars tries to block his way, so Ethan does a 720-degree gazelle flip over the front of the car. He doesn't have to do a 720-degree gazelle flip, but it just looks cool. Even the police officer is impressed.

The police cars close in. Ethan needs to do something to escape. Preferably something awesome.

Draw some **THUMBTACKS** to puncture the car tires.

Or an **OIL SLICK** to make the road slippery.

Or a **BIG HOLE** for them to fall into.

So far so good. All Ethan needs to do is get to the county line and he is safely home.

But, look, it's a **HUGE ROADBLOCK**.

Time for something drastic! Ethan reaches into his bag and pulls out...

Go to page 139 to find out what it is! Then come back and turn the page!

Now place this book on the floor and throw the paper plane over the police cars on the opposite page.

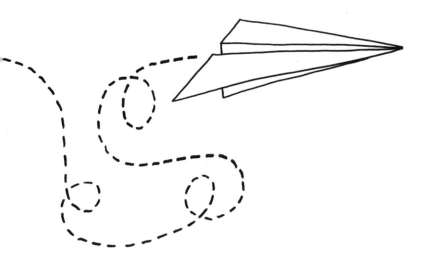

Ethan takes off and flies over the police cars. The officers stand there scratching their heads. They have never seen such an **AUDACIOUS** escape.

Except maybe the time Lenny Shrugs broke out of jail in his granny's handbag.

CHAPTER FIVE
TEDIOUS!

Ethan flies back to his **TOP SECRET SPY HQ**.
Oops! Did I write that too loudly?

Spy HQ is an ordinary building on the edge of
Doodletown, and if it were not for the big sign that
says **TOP SECRET SPY HQ**, no one would suspect
that this is where spies hang out.

Ethan parks his plane in the paper-recycling
hangar and makes his way to the entrance. He needs
a code to enter the building.

What do you mean you don't know what the
code is?

Thank goodness Ethan scribbled it down on
page 23.

Ethan punches in the code and heads straight to
his desk. He doesn't even stop to talk to his friend
Agent 99.

THAT'S how excited he is.

He turns on his evidence scanner.

PLACE EVIDENCE HERE

What evidence did you get?

☑ A photo of Mr. Flakey.

☐ A recording of Kate.

☐ A sample of Lord Byron's muffin.

Ethan leaves the evidence scanner working away and heads to his boss's office. "Hey, Chief," he says as he leans around the door. "You are never going to guess what happened to me today."

The chief is sitting behind his desk, looking at his computer. He glares at Ethan. "I have some idea."

FLY SPY SAYS BYE
MUFFIN SUSPECT IN DARING
ESCAPE FROM POLICE CUSTODY

"Oh," says Ethan. "I can explain."
"I'm listening," says the chief.

Ethan tells his story. Help him by checking the boxes.

"Well, it's like this, Chief. I was in McGuffin's Muffins this morning when the recipe went missing.

"I noticed a suspicious

☑ **MAN**   ☐ **WOMAN**

leave in a hurry so I decided to follow them.

"They tried to lose me by

☑ **DUMPING A NEWSPAPER.**

☐ **JUMPING IN A TAXI.**

☐ **GOING TO THE SUPERMARKET.**

"I managed to track them all the way across town to a

☐ **FACTORY.**

☑ **CUPCAKE SHOP.**

☐ **MANSION.**

"I got some evidence and made my way back to McGuffin's Muffins to tell Mr. Dozen, the baker, but the police were waiting. They thought I stole the recipe! They took me to the police station but wouldn't believe my story. So I had to escape to get back here with the evidence. I'm doing the forensics on it now with the evidence scanner."

"Ethan," says the chief slowly, "that sounds like a crazy story. You need to show me the evidence."

The chief follows Ethan back to his desk, where the evidence scanner has just finished its analysis.

"I think we've got a result," says Ethan, pointing to the screen.

```
C:\> ANALYSIS COMPLETE...
01  The 1st letter on page 6
02  The 4th letter on page 34
03  The 1st letter on page 56
04  The 1st letter on page 10
05  The 3rd letter on page 64
06  The 1st letter on page 50




07  The 4th letter on page 84
08  The 1st letter on page 59
09  The 2nd letter on page 10
10  The 2nd letter on page 30
11  The 1st letter on page 66
12  The 2nd letter on page 5
13  The 2nd letter on page 24
```

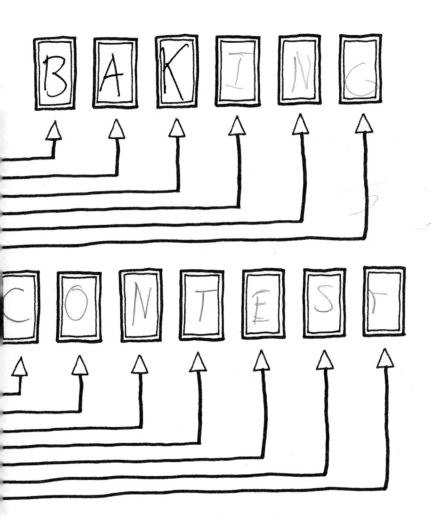

"I knew it!" says Ethan. "It's the **BAKING CONTEST**!"

Or the **BAKWIG NONTESK** if you got some of the letters wrong.

The chief stares at the screen. "Okay, Ethan, I'll give you twenty-four hours to solve this."

"Awesome!" says Ethan. "Can I use the equipment in the equipment store? Please?" The chief glares at Ethan. "Please? Please please please please please? Pleeeeeease?" says Ethan.

"Okay," says the chief. "But only because you asked nicely."

EQUIPMENT STORE

which probably sounds really boring,
except in this instance
"EQUIPMENT"
actually means

"AMAZING SPY GEAR"

and
"STORE"
actually means

"STORE!!!!!"

Ethan knocks on the door. A slot opens and a pair of eyes peers out. "What's the password?" says the mouth belonging to the eyes.

"Swordfish," says Ethan, rolling his eyes. "The password is always 'swordfish,' Stan."

Stan opens the door carefully and looks out to make sure no one else is there. "Quick. Come in," he says, ushering Ethan through.

Ethan tells Stan he needs equipment for a mission. "What sort of mission is it?" asks Stan.

"Undercover infiltration. With some jetpacking."

"Okay," says Stan, "but you have some paperwork to do first."

SPY EQUIPMENT REQUEST FORM

THE UNDERSIGNED IS GIVEN PERMISSION TO BORROW SOME INCREDIBLY EXPENSIVE SPY EQUIPMENT AND PROMISES TO:

- ☑ Not break anything.
- ☑ Not lend it to any friends.
- ☑ Not bring it to school where it could get confiscated.
- ☑ Not leave it on the bus.
- ☑ Not swap it for any trading cards.
- ☑ Not leave it in a bag with smelly old gym gear.
- ☑ Not "accidentally" drop it in a volcano.
- ☑ Not leave it lying on the sidewalk all night outside the house like that new bicycle you got for Christmas.

Please sign here: Umm_ _ _ _ _ _ _ _ _ _

Once Ethan has signed the form, he can take whatever he needs.

Help him choose his equipment and pack his bag:

Laser pen

Wirecutters

Pineapple

Laptop computer

Walkie-talkie

Phone

Pet hamster

Sandwich

Parachute

X-ray glasses

Boomerang

First-aid kit

ADD MORE ITEMS.

When all his gear is packed, Ethan realizes he will need some way of getting to the baking contest. In style.

"I need some wheels. Do you have anything cool?" he asks Stan.

"Unfortunately the DeLorean has had a time malfunction," says Stan.

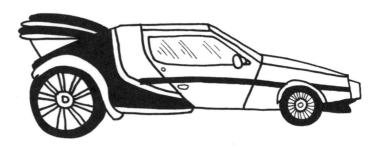

"Something armored?" asks Ethan.

"Sorry," says Stan. "The tank is being resprayed."

COLOR THE TANK PINK.

"Can I take the jetpack?" Ethan asks.
Stan looks at him. "After what you did last time?
No way."

YEEE-HAW!

Ethan sighs. He'll **NEVER** live that down apparently.
"Well, do you have anything I can use?"
"You can borrow my car, I suppose," says Stan.

Ethan and Stan stand beside a Bugatti Veyron.
Ethan looks **INCREDULOUS**. "This is your car?!"

"Sure," says Stan. "It used to be a minivan, but I
did some remodeling." He points to the dashboard.
"I've added some extras."

The chief drops by to see Ethan off on his mission.
"Remember rule forty-two of spying?" says the chief as Ethan gets into the car.

Ethan rolls his eyes and says, "Don't be conspicuous."
"Yes," says the chief, "so play it smart and don't stand out too much."

CHAPTER SIX
DISGUISE!

Ethan is driving to the baking contest. He leans out of the window of the car, blaring the stereo and shouting at everyone, "Yo! Wassup?"

Ethan thinks that everyone thinks he is **AWESOME**.

But everyone really thinks that Ethan **STINKS**.

Hey, Ethan! Remember rule 42?

No, obviously not.

There's a roadblock ahead. It's the police. They are looking for **ESCAPED CONVICT** Ethan Doodle!

Stay calm, Ethan. Don't panic.

"Aaaaaah!" says Ethan, panicking. "What am I going to do?"

This is Stan's car, Ethan. What do you think?

Go back to page 92 and check out your options.

Ethan presses one of the DISGUISE buttons. The car transforms instantly into a...

Er, wrong button, Ethan. I meant the one with the **POLICE CAR** on it.

Ethan pulls up to the checkpoint. Let's hope this disguise is convincing.

"Pull over," says the officer, waving him down.

Fingers crossed!

Ethan winds down his window. "How can I help you, officer?"

"An ice-cream cone, please," says the police officer, holding out some money.

Phew!

"Sure thing," says Ethan.

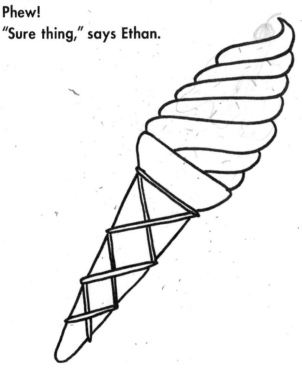

Draw some toppings on the ice cream. How about sprinkles or syrup? Or **BOTH**?

The police officer lets Ethan pass, and he goes straight to Channel 27, Doodletown's local TV station, where the baking contest is being held.

Security is tight. Ethan takes out his plan to get into the TV station and studies it.

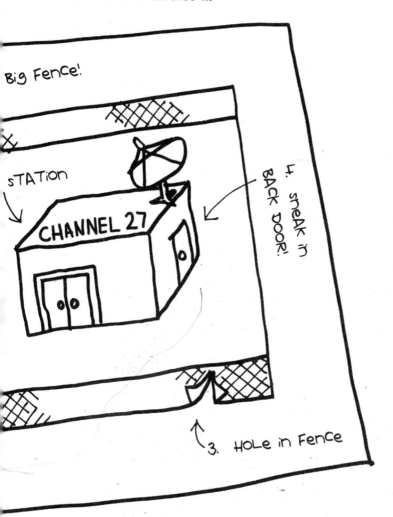

Draw Ethan's route from his car to the back door. Make sure he isn't spotted!

CHAPTER SEVEN
INFILTRATION!

Ethan makes it to the back door without getting caught.
    But the door is locked.
    He tries his master key. No luck.
    He tries overriding the security system with his computer. Not a chance.
    He considers blowing the door off its hinges. Too noisy.
    Finally Ethan looks up rule 37 in the spy manual.

Go to page 133 to find out what it is.

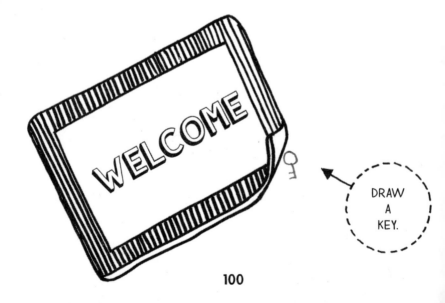

DRAW A KEY.

Ethan unlocks the door and lets himself in. He finds himself in a backstage hallway with three more doors. Which one should he open?

Does he go through this one?
Turn to page 102.

Does he open this one?
Turn to page 108.

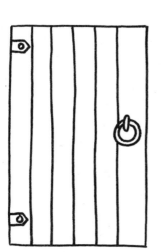

What about this door?
Turn to page 114.

"Quick, you're late! We're about to start."

Ethan has just stepped into a dressing room and has been met by an excited young woman wearing headphones and holding a clipboard.

"The show is about to start," she says. "Where have you been?"

Ethan mumbles something about the bathroom. That's **ALWAYS** a good excuse.

The young woman drags Ethan down the hallway, through another door, and past more people holding clipboards.

"This way," she says, stepping over cables that snake all over the floor. "Through here," she says, pushing him through a thick curtain. "Here we go," she says, pulling him out into a huge auditorium filled with people.

In front of the crowd is a large, brightly lit stage. There are TV cameras and lights and loud music playing. In front of the stage is a desk with three seats. Two of them are occupied. The young woman points to the third seat and tells Ethan to sit down.

It's Mary Banoffee and Paul Scone! Ethan recognizes the judges from his favorite TV show:

BAKER
OR
FAKER

"You are late," says Mary Banoffee crossly. She turns to Paul Scone. "So unprofessional."

Oh dear, it looks like they've confused Ethan with someone else!

The young woman speaks into her microphone. "We are live in 5...4...3...2...1..."

Loud music plays. The stage lights up. Ethan looks up to see three people standing in front of him, holding muffins.

Mary Banoffee speaks to the nearest camera. "Welcome back to the finale of **BAKER OR FAKER**, with our three contestants, Mr. Flakey, Kate, and Lord Byron de Doodle. We are also joined by our **MYSTERY JUDGE**, local baker Mr. Dozen."

She turns to Ethan. "Mr. Dozen, as an expert, who do you think is the winner of the muffin contest?"

The camera turns to Ethan.

Ethan stares blankly at the camera while everyone waits for him to speak. "Um..." he says. "Ah..."

"Well?" says Mary Banoffee.

The three contestants stare at him, waiting.

BAKER OR FAKER
5th ANNUAL MUFFIN CONTEST

I think the ~~winner~~ thief is:

☐ MR. FLAKEY—SAVORY SURPRISE

☐ KATE—BAKED BIG BANG

☐ LORD BYRON DE DOODLE— *CANARD* CAKE

So, who do you think is **GUILTY**? I mean, the **WINNER**?

Just as Ethan chooses, there is a shout and a flustered man runs onto the stage waving his arms.

He points at Ethan. "Stop! Stop! I am the **REAL** Mr. Dozen, and this man stole my recipe!"

Everyone turns to Ethan.

Uh-oh. **TROUBLE**.

Turn to page 120.

Ethan opens the door into a dark room filled with TV screens. It's the control room for a TV show. **AWESOME!** A producer sits at a desk filled with switches and knobs. He turns to Ethan.

"Go down to the stage right away. We are going live in five minutes," he says in a near panic. He has clearly confused Ethan for someone who works here.

"Okay," says Ethan, grabbing a pair of headphones.

108

This is **GREAT**, thinks Ethan as he puts on the headphones and runs downstairs. I'll be able to go anywhere with these on.

The headphones buzz to life and Ethan hears the producer's voice. "We're missing a microphone for one of the contestants. Figure that out **IMMEDIATELY**!"

Ethan charges out onto the stage, where the contestants are lined up for the final round of the baking contest.

The producer is right. One of the microphones is missing. Draw it as quickly as you can! The show is about to start!

Ethan's headphones buzz.

"There is a problem with Camera 3," says the producer. "Can you check out the fuse board beside the stage?"

Ethan runs to the side of the stage, where he finds a large box filled with wires and connectors.

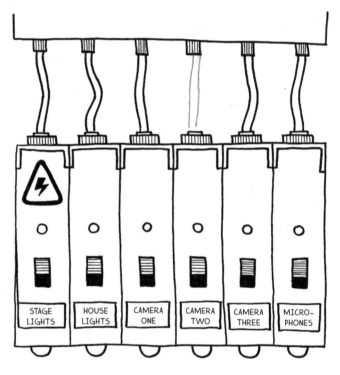

"I see the problem," says Ethan into the microphone. "The wire for Camera 3 is missing."

Draw in the wire between the switch for Camera 3 and the connector.

The producer is talking in Ethan's ear again. "I need you on stage immediately! Someone forgot to lay the track for Camera 2."

Ethan runs back to the stage. He sees that one of the cameras is running on a track. But there is a section **MISSING**!

Quick! Draw in the missing section.

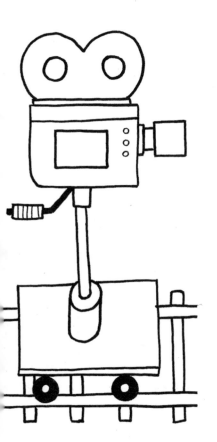

"We need another light over the stage!" shouts the producer in his ear.

This is **CRAZY**! Is anybody else working here besides Ethan?

He looks up at the lighting rig above the stage. It's **VERY** high. He runs to the ladder and starts climbing.

Up…

And up…

Until he reaches the lighting rig.

Carefully he starts to crawl out. He can see the contestants on the stage far below.

Can you help him by drawing an extra light?

UH-OH! Drawing the extra light has made the lighting rig very **HEAVY**. It starts to wobble and shake...

CRACK!

The rig snaps and starts to fall. Ethan, the lights, and the rig tumble down...

AAAAAAAAH!

And crash on to the stage in a heap...

KER-RASH!

Turn to page 120.

The door opens. Ethan steps through and is immediately blinded by bright lights. There is a very loud noise, and as his eyes adjust, he realizes it is the sound of a **HUGE** crowd clapping and cheering him.

A loud voice booms, "A big welcome to our next contestant."

As Ethan's eyes adjust to the light he sees a desk in front of him with three people sitting at it. Sitting in the spare seat with Mary Banoffee and Paul Scone is Mr. Dozen, the baker.

It's the judges from **BAKER OR FAKER**, Ethan's favorite TV show!

"Step forward, please," says Mary Banoffee to Ethan as the applause calms down. "And your name is...?"

Ethan needs to come up with a name quickly. Let's give him a suggestion.

A: What is your best friend's name? Write it in the first space below.

B: Select one of these words and write it in the second space below:

☐ CHERRY ☐ SNUFFLE ☐ NOODLE

☐ WADDLE ☐ DINKY ☐ ARGLE

C: Pick another word from the list below and write it in the third space:

☐ BOTTOM ☐ SPORK ☐ NOGGIN

☐ PANTS ☐ HEAD ☐ KISS

Ethan steps forward and says, "My name is

_____ _____ – _____ "

A: YOUR FRIEND'S NAME B: FIRST WORD C: SECOND WORD

"Well, that is certainly an interesting name," says Mary Banoffee. "Let's not waste any more time, shall we? On your marks, get set, **BAKE**!"

In front of Ethan is a table filled with ingredients that he needs to turn into a muffin of some sort.

Which ones do you think would be useful?

CHILES   MUSTARD   SUGAR

KETCHUP   PEAS   BUTTER

MILK   BANANAS   EGGS

Ethan puts all those items in a big bowl. Mmm, this should be **DELICIOUS**.

Scribble in the bowl as **FAST** as you can to mix everything.

Ethan pours the mixture into a muffin tray. The audience cheers and claps when he **DOESN'T** spill any.

"Incredible skill!" says Mary Banoffee.

"I have never seen anyone **NOT** make a muffin mess before," says Paul Scone.

AMAZING! Ethan looks like he knows what he is doing. Now all he needs to do is put the muffins in the oven and switch it on.

What temperature should he set the oven to?

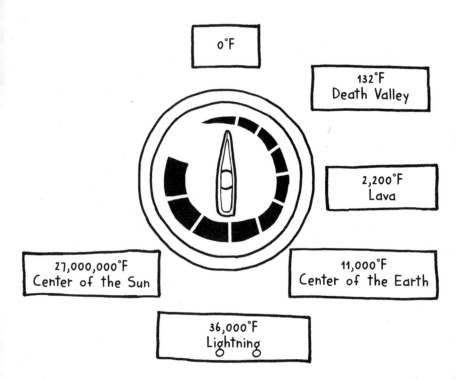

0°F

132°F
Death Valley

2,200°F
Lava

27,000,000°F
Center of the Sun

11,000°F
Center of the Earth

36,000°F
Lightning

That's **TOO HOT**! What were you thinking?

The oven bursts into flames.

Then the table catches fire.

Then the stage.

Paul Scone screams. The fire alarm starts ringing. The audience runs for the fire exits. The TV crew runs around with fire extinguishers.

Water starts spraying everywhere from the sprinklers in the ceiling.

"What have you done?" screams Mary Banoffee. "You've ruined my show and my hair!"

Well done!

Turn to page 120.

BIG TROUBLE!

Everyone looks **VERY** annoyed.

How are you going to talk your way out of this one, Ethan?

"Grab him!" says someone.

"Don't let him escape," says someone else.

"Wait!" says Ethan. "I can explain!"

The crowd closes in on him.

Ethan yells at the top of his voice, "I know who took the McGuffin muffin recipe!"

Everybody pauses and stares at him.

Ethan points at the suspect and says, "It was..."

Mr. Flakey!
Turn to page 132.

Kate!
Turn to page 142.

Lord Byron!
Turn to page 141.

Everyone starts **YELLING** and **SHOUTING**. There is total **CONFUSION**.

"He took the recipe," someone shouts.

"I took the recipe," someone yells.

"My cat has the recipe," says someone else.

A cream pie flies through the air and **SPLATS** Mary Banoffee in the face.

SCRIBBLE ALL OVER HER FACE.

Someone else throws a cream pie.

SPLAT!

Suddenly a voice cries out: **"I SAID, I KNOW WHERE THE RECIPE IS!"**

Everyone turns around in surprise.

LOOK! It's Undrawn John from page 8!

"I saw who took it," says Undrawn John. "They tore the page from the book, wrote their name on it, folded it up, and **HID** it!"

The whole crowd waits expectantly.

Undrawn John points and says, "It was..."

YOU!

"That kid reading this book tore out a page!" says
Undrawn John. "The McGuffin muffin recipe was on
the back."

Mr. Dozen, the baker, steps forward. "Well," he says, "I suppose it doesn't really matter anyway. It's not a big secret. The recipe is free on my website."

Everybody bursts out laughing. Oh, Mr. Dozen! You just wasted **EVERYONE'S** time.

"No hard feelings," says a police officer as he takes the handcuffs off Ethan.

Everyone thinks it is **HILARIOUS**.

Except Ethan.

He feels a bit foolish. "This was a very silly story," he says.

He's right too. It **WAS** a very silly story. Ethan didn't even get to use the **EXCELLENT THING** that Mr. Sonley gave him.

Ethan has a big bright smile on his face. A lightbulb goes off over his head.

"The excellent thing!" he says. "I forgot the excellent thing."

Guess what it was?

If you guessed it was a

LASER-FIRING,

DRONE-DEPLOYING,

TURBO-POWERED

STEALTH

JETPACK...

...you were **CORRECT!**

THE
END

I bet you are glad **THAT** is over.

What? You want more?

Okay. Go back to the start and...

COLOR IT ALL IN!

Mr. Flakey stares at Ethan. His face begins to turn red and he starts to shake. "What on **EARTH** are you talking about?"

COLOR HIS FACE RED.

"I saw the Man without the Newspaper give you the secret recipe that he stole from Mr. Dozen," says Ethan.

"That was a **BIRTHDAY CARD**!" says Mr. Flakey. "It was my **BIRTHDAY**!"

"But what about your muffins? Where did you get the recipe?" asks Ethan.

"I'm **MR. FLAKEY THE BAKER**," says Mr. Flakey. "Where do you **THINK**?"

Oh dear, Ethan. It looks like you made a mistake. Go to page 122.

Rule 36:
Make sure you are wearing pants.
Rule 37:
Always look under the doormat first.
Rule 38:
Remember, you are always being followed.
Rule 39:
Always cut the blue wire first.
Rule 40:
Look both ways when crossing a road.
Rule 41:
Always walk backward through snow.
Rule 42:
Don't be conspicuous.

Can't keep a secret?
UH-OH!

THIS BOOK WILL SELF-DESTRUCT IN

5...

4...

3...

2...

1...

Go to page 144.

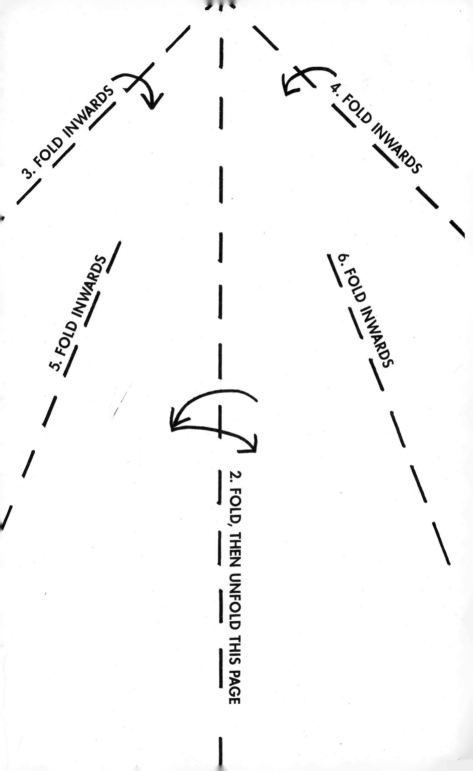

3. FOLD INWARDS

4. FOLD INWARDS

5. FOLD INWARDS

6. FOLD INWARDS

2. FOLD, THEN UNFOLD THIS PAGE

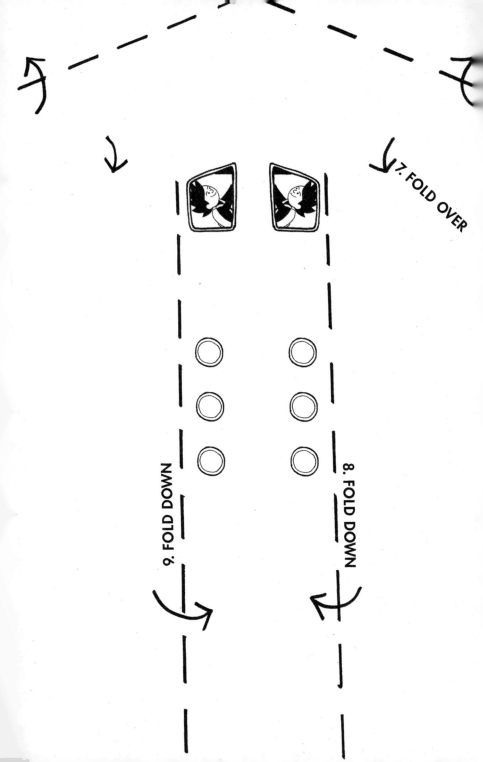

7. FOLD OVER

8. FOLD DOWN

9. FOLD DOWN

Lord Byron looks **HORRIFIED**. He tries to speak. "What...what are you saying?"

"You had written down the McGuffin muffin ingredients list," says Ethan, "even though you claimed it was for an old family recipe."

"I wrote down the list because I am **OLD**," he says. "I sometimes forget things. Is that a **CRIME**?"

Everybody **GASPS**. Ethan is picking on an innocent old man. That doesn't go over too well...

You had better get to page 122.

Kate is **SHOCKED**. She stares at Ethan. "What are you accusing me of?" she asks him.

"I saw you taking a photo of the recipe," says Ethan. "I followed you back to your cupcake shop."

"I was taking a photo of my sleeve. The spots gave me an idea for a secret ingredient: **BLUEBERRIES**!"

Oh dear, Ethan. It looks like your adventure was **FRUITLESS**.

Go to page 122.

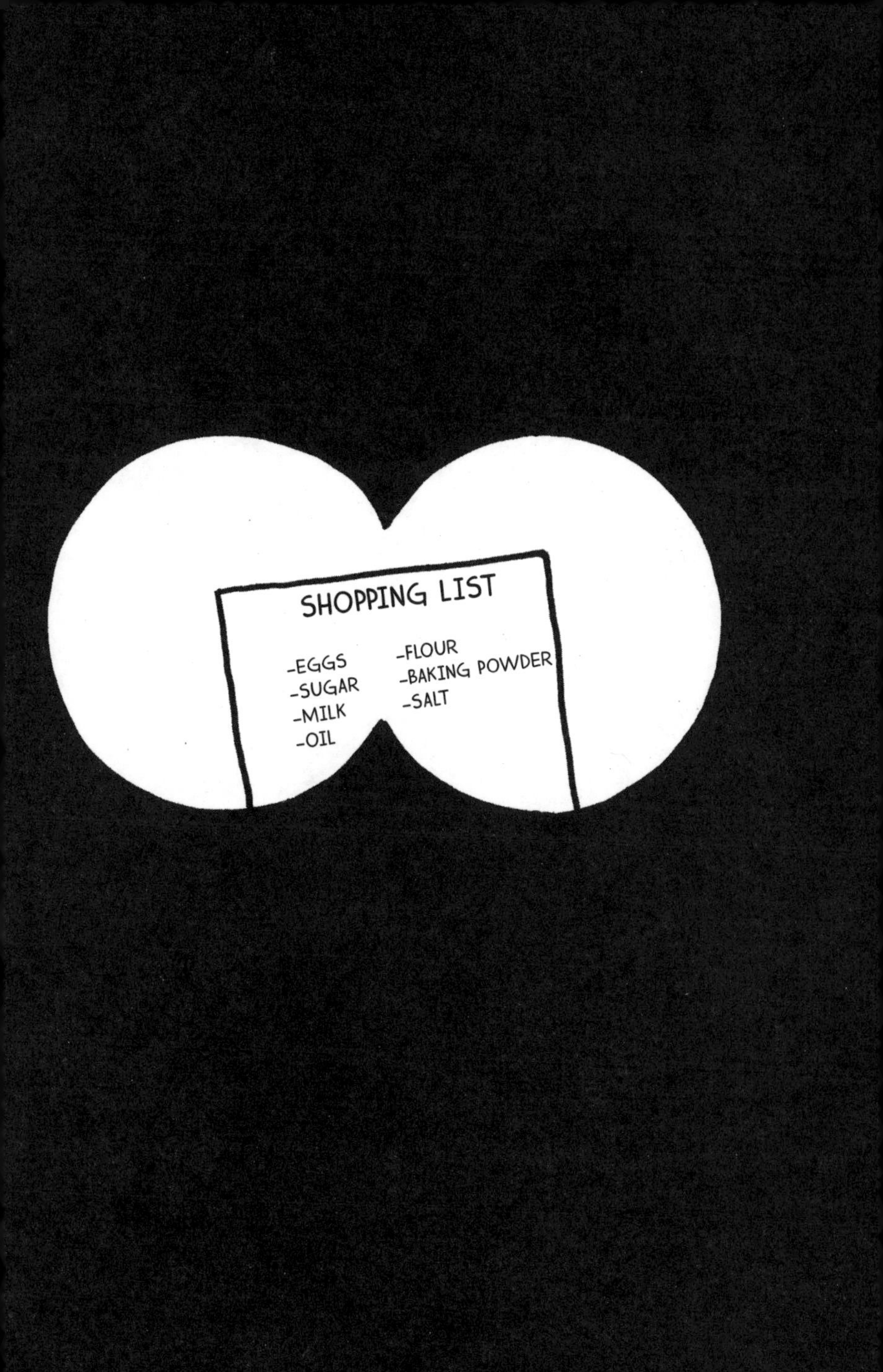
SHOPPING LIST
-EGGS
-SUGAR
-MILK
-OIL
-FLOUR
-BAKING POWDER
-SALT

THE END
Good-bye!

What? You've changed your mind?
Well, okay. Go back to page 11 then.